Soft Child

How Rattlesnake Got Its Fangs

A Native American folktale retold by
Joe Hayes

Illustrated by
Kay Sather

Harbinger House
TUCSON

For Byrd Baylor

*She leads the way
in sharing the Southwest
in stories.*

Published by
HARBINGER HOUSE INC.
P.O. Box 42948
Tucson, AZ 85733-2948

© 1993 Joe Hayes
Illustrations © 1993 Kay Sather
All rights reserved.
Manufactured in the United States of America.

⊗ This book was printed on acid-free, archival-quality paper.
Designed by Harrison Shaffer

10   9   8   7   6   5   4   3   2

Library of Congress Cataloging-in-Publication Data

Hayes, Joe.
  Soft Child : how rattlesnake got its fangs : a Native American
folktale / retold by Joe Hayes ; illustrated by Kay Sather.
     p.   cm.
  Summary : When his warning rattle fails to protect Soft Child from
the other desert creatures, the Sky God equips him with a powerful
way to defend himself.
  ISBN 0-943173-89-2 (pbk.)
  1. Tohono O'Odham Indians—Legends.   2. Rattlesnakes—Sonoran
Desert—Folklore.   [1. Tohono O'Odham Indians—Legends.   2. Indians
of North America—Legends.   3. Rattlesnakes—Folklore.]   I. Sather,
Kay, ill.   II. Title.
  E99.P25H39   1993
  398.2 ' 0899—dc20   93-1641

A long time ago, they say, the Sky God made all the animals from the sands and clay of the desert. When he had finished, he called the animals together.

"Each animal may ask for a way to protect itself," the Sky God told the animals. "I will give it to you."

Mountain Lion roared, "Give me sharp claws and teeth!"

And the Mountain Lion received sharp claws and teeth.

Skunk muttered, "Make me smell terrible. They'll leave me alone."

And Skunk smells terrible.

Jackrabbit wanted long legs, so that he could run fast and escape his enemies.

Coyote wanted to be clever, so he could trick the other animals.

Everyone knows what Porcupine wanted!

But there was one animal—a very gentle little snake—who said, "I'm only worried that s-s-someone might s-s-step on me as I go along on my belly on the ground. Can you give me a way to let the other animals know I'm down there? Then they won't s-s-step on me!"

And so the Sky God put a rattle on the end of the snake's tail. Now he could make a noise to let other animals know when he was around.

But it didn't take the other animals long to find out that even though the snake could make a noise with his tail, he was perfectly harmless. He couldn't hurt them in any way.

In fact, he was so gentle, they all called him "Soft Child." And they would pick on him just to make him rattle his tail!

Jackrabbit and Skunk were the worst. Skunk would throw Soft Child into the air. Jackrabbit would wait until he came down and then kick him back up in the air again! They would laugh and laugh as Soft Child rattled his tail.

Once there was a big ceremonial. All the animals gathered for a day of dancing. And Jackrabbit and Skunk were especially cruel to Soft Child that day. Over and over they kicked and tossed him into the air.

But the Sky God was looking down on the dancing. He saw what was going on. That evening he came down and talked to Soft Child.

"Let's go walking in the desert," he said. "I'll give you something."

They walked along until they came to a devil's claw plant. The Sky God broke the two sharp, curved points from a devil's claw and then told Soft Child, "Open your mouth."

He put those sharp points in the snake's mouth. Then he touched each point with a bolt of lightning.

"Now you have two poison fangs you can bite with," the Sky God told Soft Child.

"Your bite will be the most deadly of all. But you must promise that you'll only use your fangs to protect yourself. And whenever you can, you'll rattle your tail to warn other animals before you bite them.

Soft Child gave his promise.

The next day, Soft Child was moving along through the desert minding his own business when Jackrabbit happened to see him.

Jackrabbit said to Skunk, "Come on! Let's tease Soft Child some more."

Skunk said, "No. We teased him a lot yesterday. Let's leave him alone."

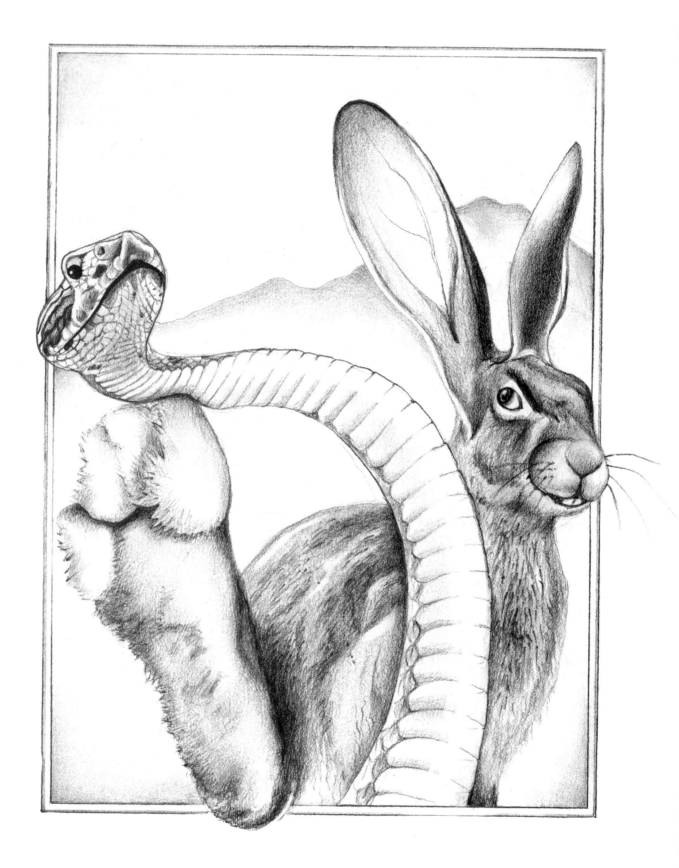

But Jackrabbit wouldn't be satisfied until he had picked on Soft Child. He ran over and kicked the snake with his hind leg. Soft Child rattled his tail.

Jackrabbit laughed and threw Soft Child into the air. The snake landed hard on the dirt.

S oft Child rattled louder, but Jackrabbit just laughed louder. He threw the snake again, and again.

But when Jackrabbit threw him a fourth time, Soft Child wouldn't take it any more. He turned on Jackrabbit and bit him with his new fangs!

All the animals were surprised to see Soft Child bite. He had never done that before.

And then when Jackrabbit fell to the sand and quivered all over, and then lay perfectly still, they said among themselves, "Stay away from Soft Child. He is deadly. He has poison fangs he'll bite you with!"

Ever since that day, the other animals have been afraid of the rattlesnake.

But the truth is, Soft Child was given his fangs to protect himself. And whenever he can he will rattle his tail to give a warning before he bites.

The people who tell this story know that. And they tell the others who are frightened of rattlesnakes, "Don't be afraid. Every creature has a place in this desert world. Just stay away from Soft Child. He won't bother you if you don't bother him."

About the Author and Illustrator

Joe Hayes, who lives in Santa Fe, New Mexico is considered to be the foremost Southwestern story-teller. His folktales and Native American stories have been heard by thousands of children and adults in the past decade. *Soft Child* has been adapted from the lore of the Tohono O'odham (Pápago) people of southern Arizona, and it is Joe's tenth book.

Kay Sather is an accomplished illustrator and graphic designer who lives and works in Tucson, Arizona. Her sensitive and scientifically accurate drawings bring forth the subtle beauty of the Sonoran desert and have appeared in numerous books and magazines, including *Tucson Guide Quarterly* and *Tucson Weekly*.

About the Tohono O'odham

The desert of southern Arizona and northern Sonora, Mexico, has been home to the Tohono O'odham (Pápago) and their close relatives the Pima for many hundreds of years. With a deep understanding of the plants and animals of the desert and of the yearly rhythm of its seasons, they managed to make a comfortable life for themselves in a land that newcomers thought harsh and unfriendly. They made dome-shaped houses from desert brush and usually attached a ramada under which they could work or rest, protected from the hot sun and cooled by every gentle breeze that stirred. They were skilled in the science of irrigation and successfully farmed the desert valleys. They hunted and they harvested the fruits and seeds of desert plants. Today, on a four-part reservation in Arizona, many Tohono O'odham preserve the wisdom and practice the ways taught by their ancestors.

Like most Native American tribes of Southwest, the Tohono O'odham have respect for snakes, rather than fear or hatred. Another tale describes the rattlesnake as a great medicine man and the sharer of much wisdom about life in the desert. It was he who first taught the people to build ramadas for protection from the desert sun. Other people believe that snakes serve as messengers between the world we live in and the spirit world that lies below this one. Many Southwestern tribes have a strong taboo against the killing of any snake.

Stories of the helpless rattlesnake being given the most deadly power of any animal because it was so abused by its fellow creatures occur in the lore of many Native American tribes, and have even been found in African American lore as well.

Of course a rattlesnake bite is very dangerous, sometimes even fatal. So when we go walking in the rattlesnake's desert home, we must be aware that we may meet him. When we do, we should keep our distance, admire the beauty of this desert creature for a while, and then go on our way.